Madmen,

Poets, &

Thieves

John Urbancik

John Urbancik

Madmen, Poets & Thieves

Audiobook version available from 7 Story Rabbit.
Narrated by John Urbancik
www.7StoryRabbit.com

Madmen,

Poets, &

Thieves

◯

Ah, but of course I remember the sun. I wasn't born in this horrible dark place, and believe me, I'll be elsewhere when I die. So yes, I remember the sun, and I remember sunrise over the ocean, so when a woman such as she walks into a room, wearing a dress the color of an ocean sunrise, with eyes like a twilight sky and hair like spider webs in moonlight—believe me, I know a mystery when I see one, and she, whoever she may be, whatever else she may claim, is one hundred percent mystery. I immediately know I must see her again, speak with her without restraint, unlock her passions and lose myself in her poisons. I'd known other women, a great many, I daresay, but the moment this mystery entered the room wearing an ocean sunrise, I forgot the names of all of them.

In fact, I can think of nothing and no one else, and can't recall why I'd been in the room in the first place, nor who else might be here. It could as easily have been a prison or a dancehall, though of course it's something bland, a restaurant, filled with a wait staff dressed quite casually. I should be surrounded by tuxedoes and capes and men with pocket watches, and certainly the woman wrapped in an ocean sunrise deserves nothing less. I gather my courage and wits from the darkest crevices within my very soul and, quite daringly, I stride across the big room and sit in the chair opposite her.

She sits alone. Such are the depths of her mystery, that she should ever be forced to dine alone except by choice. She looks at me with eyes like weapons and asks, "Do I know you?"

"Absolutely, I wish that was true," I say. "Would you allow me the chance to change the answer to an unambivalent yes?"

She does a great many things in response. She taps a perfectly painted fingernail on the edge of the table one time. Twice, she blinks, once perhaps to find meaning in my words and once more to find words to fit her meaning. She glances away, fleetingly, searching for some hidden camera or jokester or thief, but she cannot keep her eyes away.

I know it will be up to me to get this conversation started, so I say, "My name is Derek Smith, which may perhaps not sound like the most descriptive of names, except that I am, indeed, a smithy of a type. What would you prefer I call you?"

She graces me, then, with a smile, and says, "Angeline."

"Wonderful," I say. "I love a name with multiple syllables. You can change the meaning merely by adjusting your inflection and emphasis. Your mother, I believe, did you the greatest service by giving you such a wondrous name."

"You're trying my patience," she says.

Until that moment, I'd forgotten where we were. This is not my living room, or the concourse outside an opera house; this is a restaurant, and two waiters have arrived to take her order. More precisely, one has arrived to inquire if there was anything he could get her, and the other has come to be on hand should the thing she require be my removal.

"My apologies, then," I say, standing, still overcome by the ocean sunrise. "I must have mistaken you for a lover I lost in a dream." I do not, cannot, wait for a response. I flee. I go back to my table, where I take my coat and leave some coins, finish my whiskey in a single shot, and then, only after all that, I flee the restaurant.

Of course, I cannot go far. The gravity of the woman wrapped in an ocean sunrise is far too great a force to resist. I find a place to stand, where I can support my shoulders against bricks older than my bones, and think about the great poems I will write as I uncover each layer of mystery. I look up to the moon and implore her, the goddess within her or the very rock in the sky, I know not. I beg for the right words. I fear I may have already blundered, or at least put myself at a great disadvantage. I must learn to pace myself, or to think before I act, but then I wouldn't be who I am and what would be the fun in that?

Time means nothing to me. It flows and ebbs and turns back upon itself at its whim, not mine. In this City of Night, it is always nighttime, even when it is noon, so you cannot convince me to trust in a clock or a watch or a timekeeper of any sort. When the appointed hour arrives, you might say, the mystery wrapped in an ocean sunrise emerges from the restaurant, sees me in my spot across the street, and strides straight toward me. She smiles, but not in some grandiose way; it's without promise or conviction. When she's still several paces away but has captured my gaze, she says, "You waited for me." It isn't a question, so I give no answer. "You're mad."

"I might be," I admit, "but I blame you."

"You don't know the first thing about me," she says.

"I know your mother named you Angeline," I says. "I know you dined alone, though I cannot fathom why. I could have sat across from you and admired you from close up, rather than from afar."

She looks over her shoulder. "You can't see inside the restaurant from here," she says.

"But I see the memory of you perfectly fine," I say, tapping my head beside my eye. "Isn't that worth something?"

"No," she says.

"It's worth something to me," I tell her.

"You're wrong," she says. "It's nothing. It's less than nothing. It's *sad*, is what it is."

"Sad, then," I say, "is still more than nothing."

"Have you got any money?" she asks.

"As much as I need."

"Excellent," she says. "Buy me a drink."

✹

O

Never let anyone buy you a drink. You make that kind of deal, you want to be sure of the terms. You have to get what's best for you. When you allow someone to buy your drink, you're admitting they own you, or a piece of you, even if only for a little while. It could be the last little while you've got.

But when someone offers to let you buy them a drink, that's something different. That's something deeper and far more meaningful. This is no quick exchange, no tit for tat, no shallow affair. This isn't the end of the negotiations. You're in for the long haul and the hard sell and, believe me, one hell of a runaround. You're about to have your world twisted, distorted, and deranged.

So when she commands it, when she states it like you've got no choice, and it's absolutely true that you don't, there's no room for negotiation. There's only one question: in or out? This is the point in the game where the rules have already been defined, but maybe not yet revealed; this is where you put yourself, with full intention and purpose and desire and not necessarily an ounce of wisdom; this is how you suffer. And trust me, you will suffer.

I'm in. Of course I'm in. I started this, I'm going to finish it. I'm no longer sure of the playing field. This isn't the game I thought it was. Suddenly, I'm in danger, and I've always had a problem understanding danger. Always seems so shallow, don't you think?

There's one thing about bars; they are all the same. You rotate the bartenders and the staff, change out the cheap black and white flyers advertising one kind of atonal band for another, you end up with the same cheap bourbon and a fleshy crowd of lust-addled kids desperate to shred their childhoods. They hide under neon lights and mirrors and fancy names. I tell Angeline I know a place without pretense, where the sign only says *The Bar*, at the end of Whiskey Road. It's a short road, but it lives up to its name. It provides only one bar, but it is probably the dirtiest, grittiest, most realistic bar in this or any other city. They've changed it. New ownership, apparently. I don't remember the bartender, but they're interchangeable, so what does that matter? I order two double shots of bourbon with whiskey chasers. Angeline smiles, raises her glass in a toast, and throws it back like a pro.

"Two more," she tells the bartender.

I give her my best smile. I don't give that away very often. I say, "I like you."

She says, "I know."

We take our second set of drinks to a dark booth near the window. I ignore my reflection. Never liked the way he mocks me. All white teeth and glittering eyes, and always, always one day further from his last shave than me.

"You haven't got a lot of time," she tells me.

"Time," I say, "is meaningless here. We're in Midnight." The city's named for a time, and it's always nighttime, except when the sky goes blood red for dawn and dusk. I don't bother to tell her these things; she knows.

But she says, "I decide when and if and where."

Before she gets too far, I say, "I decide how and why."

She flashes her teeth at me. "Fair enough." She finishes another drink and asks, "What do you want to know?"

"Anything," I tell her. "Everything. I want to know what makes you sing in the shower. I want to know when you stole your first lollipop. I want to know where you're from and where you're going and why. More than anything else, I want to know why." I run away with it. I'm not restricting my answer to the things I want to know about her. Life's too short for limitations. "I want to know where to catch the bus in Bermuda, and where it will take us."

"We'll never get to Bermuda," she tells me.

I laugh. "I don't care."

"And if I lie to you?" she asks.

"Then I'll be encouraged."

"And if I tell you only truths?"

"I'll be encouraged," I say.

She leans closer and narrows her eyes to deliver a line that hurts. "And if I turn you away?"

I don't answer immediately, but I am at least honest. "Then I go away."

"That's all it would take?"

"I might ask you to reconsider," I say.

"And why should I do such a thing?"

I lean back. There is no question like *why*. Answers need not be complete, nor straight, nor comprehensible. In real life, the best answer, the only answer, is *why not?* But you have to weigh the situation. This is not the time for such an answer. She wants me to work, and she wants to work herself, but she doesn't want some pop psych response anyone can parrot. I say, "I'll write you a poem."

"I don't need another poem."

"It's not strictly about need," I tell her.

She licks her lips. She's the predator here. I never had a chance. "Show me."

✸

O

We make love like fireworks, vibrantly, raucously, with a full orchestra and a drunken, cheering crowd on both sides of the river. There's no river in Midnight, and no crowd in my living room, and no sounds we don't make. She's delicious and energetic and insatiable and completely unleashed. By the time it's over, I'm out of breath, we're coated with sweat, and we need whiskey to calm ourselves. I always have a bottle or five in the kitchen.

She thumbs through the books on my shelves. She learns everything about me. She whispers promises we both know she'll never keep.

"The moon and the stars," she tells me.

But I don't want the moon.

O

We sleep late on the living room floor. When I wake, I leave her sleeping, naked and beautiful, to get my notepad. I scribble words that make no sense. I find it hard to compose. I craft something short but inexpressive. I find expression and sensation, but it's verbose and unfocused. In total, I find maybe two good words, two excellent and pliable words, but they're useless on their own so I rip out all of this morning's pages and crumple them into a ball.

From the floor, Angeline says, "No."

I shake my head. "It's a failed attempt," I tell her.

"What, can I not know your failures?"

I hand over the paper. She unrolls the pages, reads them thoroughly and thoughtfully. She flips through them, rearranges in her own head the things I've failed to write, plays with my words and phrases and emotions, and finally nods. "You're right. This is crap." She crushes it and tosses it aside. The street light through the window hits her just right, highlighting the arc of her neck, her jawline, her cheekbone. I want to make poetry. Or love.

This doesn't happen to me every day.

O

There's a place for poets and wordsmiths and rhymers and tale tellers. It's always smoky, and it's always dark, except on stage in the spotlight. It never closes, and the floor is always open, so you can bring your tambourine and sing anytime you want. I listen a lot. I'm always looking for a word to steal. There's got to be one perfect word. I've never run across it. I've used fantastic words. I've bent phrases into useful and implausible shapes. But I've never found perfection. I know why. It's not just the voice in which you write, but the voice by which you read, recite, serenade. The real problem is: you can only discover perfection through failure.

I sit in my corner with a line of empty shot glasses in front of me. They can't all be mine. A girl with long, thin hair and hollow eyes, speaking softly into the microphone, tries to tell me about lost loves and lost souls and lost ways. She hasn't ever lost her way. She's all of nineteen and thinks she's seen the world. She's never even seen the sun.

No one in Midnight will ever see the sun.

She's dull, but patient, which cannot possibly be a good combination. She wants to cry up there, but she doesn't dare ruin her makeup. Her words haven't got the depth. I know when she's finished because there's a quick round of lackluster applause.

The waitress brings me another shot glass. God, I love that woman. She keeps me in line, and in fluidity. She throws me a wink when she thinks she can get away with it. She thinks she's safe with me. She's not. She's just smarter than me, is all. I say thanks, and she calls me something condescending like hon or slick or pal. I know she doesn't mean it.

The girl sits across from me. I feel like I might fall into those hollow eyes. I try to lean back without being offensive. I'm not afraid of being offensive. I'm afraid of losing my balance. She says, "You didn't like it."

"What's not to like?" I ask.

"Everyone else, they tell me how beautiful my poems are."

"They lie."

"I know."

I smile. "Buy me a drink?"

She does. She buys for the two of us. She says, "I need you."

"No, you don't," I tell her.

"My poems need you."

"Your poems need life," I tell her. "Live."

"I can't."

"Why not?"

"I'm afraid."

"Good. Be afraid," I say. "There's lots to fear. Life can suck sometimes. It's okay. It gives you strength. Be afraid, but do it anyway."

"I've never seen you up there," she tells me.

I smile. I shrug. I say, "I have nothing to say."

"I don't believe you."

"You shouldn't," I tell her. "I lie."

"You're playing with me," she says.

"You tell me you need me, and then say I'm playing with you? What makes you think I've got anything to give you? What makes you think I know what I'm talking about?"

"You don't know a thing," she says. She's not mean about it. "I just need you to tell me when I'm going in the wrong direction."

"Fine," I say. "You're going in the wrong direction."

"And to point me in the right."

"Ah." I nod. I drink my drink. "That's the trick, isn't it?"

"I need to know if I'm real," she tells me. She's pleading. She's begging. She's reaching across the table and gripping both my wrists tightly enough to leave bruises. I don't remember losing my hands to her. I'll have to give her extra points for that.

"What's your name?" I ask.

"Ivy."

"Given, or chosen?" I ask.

She doesn't know how to smile. She's sad, but she's bored with sad. She says, "Given and chosen."

I say, "It's a good name."

◖

Later, in my living room, entangled with Angeline the way we should be entangled, blissfully happy, I say, "She wants me to teach her."

"About poetry?"

"About life."

Angeline grins at me in the dark. She traces her perfectly red fingernail down my chest, forging a new rivulet in a map to nowhere. "I don't think you know the difference."

"I did," I admit. "Once."

"You think that matters?"

I shake my head. It's hard to concentrate when Angeline's lips are so close. I feel the breath of every word on my neck. I'm intoxicated by her. I ask, "Are you jealous?"

"I don't own jealousy," she says. "I own you."

◐

I don't hear voices. I don't read secret messages off the sides of cereal boxes. I don't believe in gypsy magic any more than you do. So if an omen presents itself to me all wrapped in frilly ribbons and bows, I'll rip apart the paper like an eager, greedy Christmas child. But I might not see past the shiny bells. I might hear nothing but whistles. If there's some mystical talent for foresight, I do not have it. I sometimes have trouble with hindsight, which is less remarkable by far yet equally as impressive. It all comes down to patterns, doesn't it? And some patterns, let's face it, make your eyes hurt.

I've been owned before, in a variety of ways. There are numerous meanings to the word. I've been beaten, defeated, bought, sold, bartered, lied to, and on both the giving and receiving end of confessions. I have faults. I have failings. I have perfect recall of the present, and I remember names better than most. Names are, after all, extremely important. Ask any magician, even the ones who lie. Especially the ones who lie; I dare you to find any other type.

So when Ivy says, "I didn't see it coming," I have to admit, neither did I.

It, in this case, is the kid on the stage, the one who's got words pouring out of his mouth like showers of emeralds and diamonds. I like sharp words. I should use more. I scribble some of his into my notepad. I say nothing to Ivy. She sits too close to me, on the same side of the table, close enough to press her right arm to my left, which I don't need except to hold down the notepad. And she's buying the drinks.

The words in my notepad are meaningless jumbles of mismatched syllables, broken phrases, crooked thoughts, and empty revelations. The kid talks fast. I can't keep up. More than once, he steals entire lines from other languages. I'm crying. My hand aches from the ferocity. Ivy lays her head on my shoulder; I don't know who she's trying to comfort. I can't shrug her off. Everyone thinks she's mine and I'm hers. It might be true, in a way. But no one, not even Ivy, knows about my secret love.

The kid's got short hair and wide eyes. He's got a glass of whiskey in his hand, but I haven't seen him lift it. He's reciting his words from memory, or he's making them up on the spot. If he's that good, I should book the Suicide Penthouse at the Midnight Towers and take a dive. He's got his eyes closed, and his lips are like angel's lips, so I've got several layers of jealousy crashing around inside. I've never looked as delectable as he must. I can't see him in that way, but I can see how he can be seen. I'm not blind.

"I had no idea," Ivy says.

"Shut up and listen." Maybe I'm a little harsh, but that's what she wants from me—what she needs from me. That's why she's hanging on me like the last leaf on a winter oak. She won't let go, but one strong wind might knock her away.

The kid is one mighty strong wind.

"What's his name?" I ask.

Ivy says, "Evan."

Evan. Damn. That's a nice name. No hard consonants like Derek. It flows off the tongue. Another reason to hate him.

Ivy sighs next to my ear. Her hand clutches my thigh. When did that happen? I never noticed before. She likes what she hears. It's exciting. She's taking it out on me. There's no way this will end well.

Eventually, the kid leaves the stage, as all prodigies must. He disappears into the dark, probably kidnapped by groupies or cultists or freaks. I keep wasting ink in my notepad. I keep wasting words and pages and ideas. I have good ideas. I have horrible execution.

What's the deciding factor? What makes the kid such a force on that stage? Is it his damn lips? His throat? The words he extracts from his intestines?

"I want to write a poem," Ivy whispers. I look into her brown, beseeching eyes. I slide my notepad across the table and offer my pen. She takes it, she kisses the side of my mouth as a thank you, and she does a bit of scribbling of her own.

She bites the side of her lip as she writes, sucks it into her mouth like she's drawing words from flesh. She concentrates so hard on the paper, there should be lasers. There should be tiny black smoking holes on the paper. She twirls her fragile, thin hair with the hand that doesn't write, a nervous gesture that accomplishes nothing, a repetitive motion to keep her occupied. It's unconscious, constant movement like that that keeps her so skinny.

She doesn't scribble, doesn't spew ink like vomit onto the page. She writes tiny and tight, and when she crosses something out it's with a single, elegant line through the middle. She wields the pen like a dagger, like a weapon sprung in the dark, in close range, slid beneath the ribs when your victim thought it was all posturing and empty threats. I see a word or two that I like, and say so. She smiles but otherwise ignores me, as she should. I can't teach her anything. I don't know what she expects.

No one's on the stage. It's quiet, except for the drinking and the smoking and the under-the-breath chatter that always fills this place. Ivy adjusts the microphone to the right height, then calmly, shyly, reads the words she's written. They're good words, but they're not great, and she doesn't know enough about inflection to embolden what she's written. There's some random clapping when she's done. I smile. I always smile. I like smiling almost as much as grinning; but they're not the same thing.

"Nice," I say.

"You lie."

"No. But I don't tell the complete truth."

"What was I missing?"

"Tone," I say. "Inflection. Meaning. It wasn't about you."

"Should it be?"

"Even when it's not, yes."

She crowds in next to me, asks my goddess of a waitress for another round of whiskey, and says, "What would I do without you?" She overvalues me. I've given her nothing. I have nothing to give.

I visit my father's grave. I can't see the actual burial plot. It's in another city. You can't get there from here. But there's a big cemetery next to the Mirage, that big green park, all those trees growing without the aid of sunlight. I'll never understand. My father's grave, back home, is an anonymous, nearly blank piece of granite, a hole in which his bones slowly become ash and dust. So in this Mirage cemetery, I long ago chose an anonymous, nearly blank slate and named it my father's. He either hears me or he doesn't, wherever I go.

I talk to my father a lot. Makes up for the times we didn't talk when he was alive. I start the way I always start. "I wish I had something to say."

He speaks to me through a crow that alights upon the tomb. "You've never had something to say."

The crow is black and small. It looks at me with one eye at a time. It preens. It listens.

"Why do you always have to use a crow?" The crow, my father, doesn't answer. Why should he? It's too obvious. "I met a girl." Silence. "She's like me. Adventurous."

"Self-destructive?" the crow asks.

"No."

"Then not like you."

"I didn't have to be this way," I tell the crow, my father. "I'm actually quite happy."

"You've never been happy."

"You're not happy unless I'm not happy."

The crow bristles, adjusts its wings, looks at me with the other eye. My shadow doesn't fall across my father's stand-in grave. There are no shadows in a City of Night. It's all shadows here.

I tell my father, "We weren't done. You didn't have to die."

The crow flies away. Damn crow. I cross myself, mutter some prayer I don't really remember from Catholic school, then leave. I wipe my eyes with the back of my fist. I never learn anything from my father. I never learn.

"Roses?" Angeline asks.

We're walking. The park is cold and silent and empty. The paved path winds aimlessly and randomly. There's a cart selling caramel apples, candied apples, oversized pretzels. There's another cart selling roses. Red, pink, white, yellow, orange. A whole range, all in bloom, all challenging me to make a move.

It's a precarious situation. I can't read Angeline's tone. She's surprised. Anxious. Anxious that I'll buy her a rose, or that I won't? I buy two, one red, one white. I give the red one to Angeline.

"This is dangerous," she tells me.

"What isn't?"

"What do you want?" she asks.

It's another open ended question. She might have a specific answer in mind. I don't know it. I say, "I want the moon to shine more brightly at night. I want the sun to crest over the top of that mountain and laugh at us. I want sand and coconuts."

"Don't go predictable on me," she says.

"I want world peace," I tell her. "I want all the reins to all the horses of all the kings. I want wooden puppets and chocolate drops and vivid, sweet oranges that drip their juices down my hand and wrist and forearm when I tear them open. I want poetic armaments with which I can vanquish my enemies."

"You have no enemies," she tells me.

I look her in the eye. I challenge her to hold my gaze. I say, with my eyes, which can say a great many things at once, that I love her and need her and want her, that I fear her and will reject her, that I cannot give her what she wants, that she doesn't know what she wants at all, that the city is only as stale as its residents who are its lifeblood and its cancer both. I tell her, with my eyes, that she knows nothing about me. With my voice, with my softest whisper, I admit, "I have enemies."

Then I ask, more loudly, to prove what's been said is now behind us, "Would you like to know a secret?"

"I know many secrets," she tells me.

"Would you like one of mine?"

She blinks. She's met my gaze, she's met my challenge, she's won my game. She says, "Yes."

"I know where there's a window that can take us away from here. It's a high window, a tall window, narrow and fragile and frightening, but it's not a window, precisely, in that it's a doorway. And it's not a doorway, precisely, in that it's a mirror. And it's not a mirror, not at all, though it is in every way that matters and many ways that don't. This mirror, this window, this doorway, can lead us home again."

She reveals another secret. "You can always go home."

That's when my father, the crow, laughs. I didn't even see him until then. He takes off, leaves his lamppost, leaves me there on the dark, dirty streets, abandons me once again to wolves and tigers and myself.

✳

I give the white rose to Ivy. It might take her a while to understand. I may be part of her past by then, or she part of mine. Smoke curls around the poets trudging to the stage, one at a time, a line of them drunk on whiskey or relaxed by scarlet. I tried one of those little red pills alone in my living room. I woke up in an office with a day job, a retirement plan, a boss who liked me, a co-worker who despised me, and a coffee mug. It was the strangest thing. I found myself surrounded by blue tinted cubicle walls with a spreadsheet and less than half a clue. They gave me a paycheck. I lost three months. Never trust a drug that puts you out of your head for three months.

They recite or read or rearrange words they found or borrowed or stole. Ivy takes notes. She still sits too close. She likes me. She thinks I can offer insight and critical analysis and profundity.

I scribble in my notepad. It's tactile. The scratch of pen on paper, the sweet aroma of creative ambition wafting amid the cigarette smoke and cloves and vanilla perfumes and various spices combine to lead me down well-trodden paths. But there's a turnoff, there, maybe, or here, or right beside me.

Ivy lights a cigarette. She has a Zippo lighter she got from a pawn shop near Whiskey Road. She wrote a poem about it. I don't know why. She started smoking a week or a month ago because she thinks the ash will help her concentrate. She thinks it makes her look good. Rings of smoke rise from her fingers, and tendrils seep through her nostrils and eyes. She squints now. Did she always squint? She asks, "Have you ever written a perfect poem?"

"No one can write a perfect poem," I tell her.

"That's not true."

"Of course it's true. It's the truest thing I've ever said."

She's shaking her head. "I can't believe that."

"There's no such thing."

I'm shattering the walls of her foundation. She refuses to listen, so I sneak in more deeply. "You can write a poem that's perfect for you, and perfect for the moment, and perfect for the image, but how can it possibly be perfect for someone else who's never experienced that moment, who's not been inside your flesh and mind? You can make me know, but you can't make me change. A perfect poem would do that. A perfect poem would be perfect for everyone all the time in every way."

"That's too much," she says.

"Aiming for perfection is a madman's game," I tell her.

"You have to help me."

"You have to help you."

"I can't."

"Then I can't."

"You can't?" she asks. "Or you won't?"

The waitress saves me. She's a godsend. She's an angel. She brings fresh glasses. The line in front of me seems thin. I frown. I frown in an exaggerated way. The waitress touches my shoulder as she walks away, whispers a promise most fluid. I think she owns the place. I think she's a failed wordsmith. I think she knows the things Ivy thinks I know. I think her name is Ann, but it's not.

Ivy's still looking at me. She actually expects an answer. She's got that cigarette in one hand, the white rose in the other, squeezing both so tightly she's dropping ash on the table and the thorns bite the insides of her closed fist. Blood drops run down her wrist, her arm, hit the leg of my jeans one at a time.

Her eyes reveal nothing and everything. She hasn't found herself yet. She thinks she will turn a corner and discover the self she's always known lived inside her. But you don't find yourself; you build yourself. And her foundation, we already know, is fragile and hollow as her eyes. She searches for answers in mine.

"We have to get out of here," I tell her.

Air is a wonderful thing. From the rooftops, we look down like gods on a throbbing city in constant upheaval. The mountains still rise above, but the buildings plunge deep into the earth, deeper than we can see, and their tendrils, their alleys and lanes and apartments and courtyards, stretch outward and inward, into the hearts of the mountains, to the very edge of the forest.

Outside, beyond the walls and the edges, even the forests are constant activity, signs of motion ebbing this way and that, the self-proclaimed gypsies and sinners and thieves, the righteous and the exiled, moving in and out of the city as if boundaries don't exist.

I lean over the edge and look down. Ivy pulls me back. "I can't lose you," she says. "I have too much to learn."

I grin. "You can't lose me," I say. Gravity will never have her way with me. Nor light. I'm on the edge of shadow, and I cannot fall. She hasn't learned anything.

"I'm afraid," she says.

"Fear inhibits," I say. "Or it emboldens. Which does it do to you?"

Meekly, she admits, "It inhibits."

"Don't let it."

"How do I not?"

I tell her stories about the Monkey Man, living on the rooftops, hopping from here to there, never touching the ground, feeding off the birds, drinking the rain. I tell her about the Bird Man, living on the rooftops, flitting from there to here, never going inside, scavenging for food, drinking the rain. I tell her about the spiders and the snakes and the whippoorwill I've never seen but hear all the time. The crow, my father, perches on an antennae; I don't tell her about him.

I'm telling her about the Shadow Man, living under the streets, sneaking from here to there, never surfacing, scavenging and killing and thieving and hiding, tapping into the underground pipes so he can drink our water, when it becomes apparent she's not my only audience. There's also the crow, my father, silently judging and finding me failing. But there's another, a shape, a shadow, not the Shadow Man because we're too high above the ground, yet someone I recognize. Someone I should recognize. Someone I should, perhaps, fear.

I've been the Monkey Man and the Bird Man and the Shadow Man. I've soared above the city where the clouds go red at the change between night and day. I've prowled the alleys. I've breathed stagnant air in underground tunnels no man has seen in a hundred years or more. I've saved and slain. I've prayed. I've listened at the feet of the Wandering Reverend and discerned the truths from the lies. I've practiced the blackest of magic. I've told the worst of lies, and also the greatest. I've killed a man with the pen in my pocket. He deserved it. I'd do it again. But I've never known fear, never understood the dark or the heights. I've winked at death because everyone winks at death, you can't get away from winking at death, it's a thing death requires and demands, and though I may be a great many things I'm not so foolish as to ignore death's wishes.

I stare at the man in the shadows, the man on the rooftop. I stare until Ivy stares.

He steps out of the darker shadow and into the lighter shadow. This City of Night provides nothing but shadows. The crow, my father, positions himself for a better view.

"Your words," the man says, holding out a hand, asking for more.

"I gave them to her, not to you."

He grins. "I admit, I stole the gist of them. I'm sorry."

"You're apologizing?"

"I am."

"No one apologizes," I say. "That can't be sincere." Yet it seems like it is.

"My name's Robin," the man says. He's not moving anymore. I don't think he's looked at Ivy even once. "Rob, if you prefer."

"What do you prefer?" I ask.

He grins. He grins like I grin. I like that. Now I understand fear. He says, "I don't."

"Derek," I admit. "Derek Smith."

He tilts his head. "Ah," he says. "The poet," he says. "The poet's son," he says.

He knows me. In the space of two minutes, he knows me more completely and thoroughly than Ivy will ever know me. His eyes aren't hollow at all. His eyes are wicked. His eyes are mischief.

She's wrapped in ocean sunset the next time I see her. She's let her hair down and her eyes gleam. The dress is cut low, the heels are high. She's dressed for a funeral, but without the black. "It's time," Angeline says.

I protest.

"I've got another life to live," she tells me. We all do.

"I'm not who I was," she tells me. Who ever is?"

"This isn't the end," she tells me.

"Of course it is."

"It's not," she says. Now who's protesting? She says, "It's time, is all. To move forward or move on."

"There's a difference?"

"Of course there is. Decisions must be made."

"No," I say. "Decisions are misguided far too often."

"Remember, *when* is my purview." Yes, I ceded *when*; but I held onto *why* and I held onto *how*. Apparently, that doesn't matter. "It was the rose, of course."

"The red rose?" I ask.

"The white." Like a dagger, of course. I knew it then. I know it now. The colors make flowers mean something different, but can't change the fact of the rose. I haven't learned any of this woman's mysteries. I haven't resolved my own paradoxes. I'm irredeemable. I'm out of step.

"You're bound in too many ways," she says.

"You've become serious," I tell her.

"I've always been serious," she says. Even when she wasn't, she was serious about it. I know this now. I don't understand it. I can't focus that sharply.

We're in the bar again, on Whiskey Road, double shots and chasers set on the table between us like an alcoholic wall. Smoke obscures her features. Dark lights cast her in chiaroscurist color.

I say, "Okay." I've always been willing to risk the things no one else will risk. I tempt the shadows. I dare the shadows to expose themselves to me. I have faith in my own skills, my own weaknesses. I crawl amid the dark every day and night. I am the shade in the dance. I am the blade in the ribs. I am not afraid. "Okay," I say again. "I'm in. I'm all in."

I see the surprise on her face. The shadows hide it quickly. "You are?" The words spill out like ink.

"Isn't that what you want?"

"It's not what I expected."

"You should know me better," I say.

"I thought I did."

I shake my head. I throw back my drink. I take her hand and kiss it gently and lean over the table. I whisper. Whisper trumps shadow every time. It's like that children's game. Shadow covers secret—or shadow covers knife, I never quite remember. Knife cuts whisper. It must be a knife. Secrets can only cut when they fail to remain secrets. Knife cuts whisper. Whisper trumps shadow. When you scream, you lose all the subtlety and all the strength of the whisper. When you holler, you give up control, you put yourself in a bad place. When you whisper, you shatter secrets. You leave your mark. I lean close enough to whisper, so that my lips brush her ear, my breath warms her flesh. It means more when I whisper it. "I'm all in."

She grabs me by the back of the head, holds me close, kisses me softly, kisses me roughly, and whispers, "I'll need a ring."

I have no diamonds. But I know someone who does. In a whisper, I promise.

The band's signer is a pixie-like blonde from some beach city in another world. She hasn't seen the sun in ages—there's no sun to be seen in Midnight, and the moon does nothing for your tan—so she's brilliantly pale. Dressed all in black, the only color is around her eyes. The eyes themselves, they're as hollow as Ivy's eyes, and as dark in the center, but she paints red between her eyes and her brows, or blue, or yellow, depending on the night. Tonight it's red. Tonight, her eyes match her lips, and otherwise she's all stark shadow. She can't pull it off. Her words, her tone don't have the sorrow. She's a sun worshipper without a god, but she doesn't know melancholia the way she wants to know it. So her songs sound trite and pretty and vacuous.

"I think she's wonderful," Angeline says.

The band's drummer knows what he's doing. He's been around. He can play rock and jazz, hard and soft, quick and slow. He can pound out a melody. His eyes are cracked, like his skin. He's older than he is, and he'll die much sooner than he should. It's the drugs, the miles, the music. How he ended up backing the waif, I can't imagine. It's not up to me to imagine. He's a percussive god. I say so.

Angeline agrees.

The bass is so powerful, it swallows the player. He or she makes it do things it should never do, and makes it do these things beautifully. I once dreamt of music like that in New Orleans or Memphis, but those places are a long way from this place. Anyhow, it's the instrument playing the player. I can't recall the musician's face even as I look straight at it.

The violin is sad but shallow, broken, uncertain. He's got some skills, he does, but he doesn't believe it. That's his problem. He plays it like a guitar, like a fresh lover, like a blind man who can suddenly see. He's almost got it. He almost pulls the discordant sounds together, almost makes the song live.

"He keeps missing a note," Angeline says, but she doesn't know which.

I don't remember where we are, or what time it is. I know it's nighttime. It's always nighttime. I know the band has been playing all night, will play deep into the morning so long as there's someone here to hear them, and I'm sure we're not alone in the club. But there are mirrors, smoke and shadows, and spotlights that pick out all but one of the players. The violinist skips a note. The singer fumbles over her words, frowns, picks up where she left off. Someone—see, I told you we weren't alone here—someone cheers her on. She doesn't acknowledge him. She looks, instead, at me, as though she's only just seen me.

Angeline snakes her hand over my shoulder, up the nape of my neck, so she can turn my head to hers. She demands that kind of control. She says, "Do you love me?"

I try to be honest. "I've never known any greater love."

After the band has packed its instruments and the bar has spewed us out onto the streets, Angeline asks, "Do you love me?"

I try to be honest. "I've never known any greater love."

Submerged in my apartment again, jazz on the stereo, whiskey on the rocks, sweat on our bodies, streetlight spilling in through the windows, Angeline asks, "Do you love me?"

I try to be honest. I say, "Yes."

●

I go to my mother.

She sits on a plain wooden chair in the center of the room. A spotlight falls on her from above. She's the star of her own cabaret show, except that she doesn't sing and she doesn't dance. She sits, arms draped over the plain wood, eyes sullen and lonely and unfocused. Ink stains her cheeks. She's been crying. Her eyes are red and puffy. So are her ankles. Her lips are red. She kissed my forehead with that mouth, when I was a kid, when I fell from a fence, when another boy on the playground pushed me down in the rocks.

My mother brought me here after my father died. I don't blame her. She didn't know. A missed road sign, a wrong turn, suddenly you're in Midnight instead of Cincinnati. That's how it happens. You blink one time too many, you find yourself in another land.

I can't leave this place while she's here. I can't take her with me when I go. I will die on the streets of another, faraway city, but she will die here, in this room, in this facility, in this asylum. They keep her sedated. They keep her quiet and soft. They keep her, because I cannot.

They give me an identical chair so I can sit across from my mother, so I can keep her eyes at a level, so she doesn't have to strain herself. I say, "Mom."

She doesn't always know I'm here. She glances toward the window, the one with the iron bars. The crow, my father, looks in on us. I can't tell if he approves. There's light, like sunlight, pushing through the window, falling on the floor in a grid, but it's tinted sodium yellow, it's harsh and unrelenting.

I say, "Mom."

She doesn't move. She doesn't look at me. She doesn't try to get up. She never speaks anymore, but sometimes she whispers. With her honey velvet drawl, she says my name. "Derek."

"I'm here, mom."

She's already not listening. So I tell her anyway. I tell her I've met a girl, a living poem, flesh fashioned from my dreams. She's smart and strong, all the things a mom likes to hear. The crow, my father, laughs. Fresh ink spills from the corners of my mother's eyes. They stain her cheeks blue, just like her fingertips, her dull and cracked nails, just like the veins crawling down the length of her arms.

I tell her I'm teaching another girl. This one hasn't lost her way, she's never known her way, she may never find a way, but she's eager and anxious and I might as well teach someone.

My mother whispers. "Another girl." It's a question, without the strength of a question. She raises her eyes just enough to meet mine, just enough to focus for a fraction of a second. She sees me. She smiles. My mother has the loveliest smile. She says, "You want something."

I'm losing her already. I say, "Yes." She doesn't ask what. She drifts back to her world. Maybe it's Cincinnati. I wouldn't know. I've never been there. Neither has she. I ask, because I have to ask. I doubt she'll hear me. "I want to give her a ring."

My mother doesn't respond. The crow, my father, squawks his disapproval. "I've seen this girl," he says. "I've followed her when you weren't with her. I've seen the things she does. You're making a mistake."

I glare at the crow, my father, who cannot hear me through the window. "She's my mistake to make."

The crow, my father, shakes his head. "You never learn."

My mother whispers, "My ring."

She's slipped it off her finger. It's diamond. It's not large. It's not overpowering. It's the last thing my father gave her, the only thing my father gave her. He never gave either of us anything. My mother was always the voice. My mother was always the heart. My mother cries tears of ink and, long ago, set down my path before me. My mother slips the ring off her finger and lets it drop to the floor. It crashes like a brick. It scratches the fake tile.

I kneel before my mother to retrieve the ring. I kiss her forehead. I say, "Thank you, mom." But she no longer looks at me, or at anything. She's looking inside. The gears of her mind have been kicked again into action. She's composing poetry no one will ever hear or read.

●

Evan's poeticizing again. He must spend hours memorizing the words, the rhymes, and the metaphors, because he's not reading them. He's making eye contact. He's connecting. He's speaking to every individual soul in the place. His contact is brief, but the words are melodious and fucking deep. I'm awed. I'm captivated. I'm enthralled. And I hate him, with everything I am, because he seems to know something I only pretend to know. Ivy feels it. She must. She's neither stupid nor untalented. Her ears force the connections her mind can't make on its own.

We're not alone. There's a dozen other poets, two dozen hangers-on besides, and the waitress who smiles for me her secret smile. I think she owns me. I think she knows it. I think she knows better.

But we're really not alone. In the opposite corner, the yang to my yin, the white to my black, the disruption to my sweet and pleasant garden, Robin sits, Rob if you prefer, listening and passing judgment and pretending I'm not here. He smokes the same brand of cigarette as Ivy. Her pack floats on the table, on our side of the line of empty whiskey glasses. The fortification stands weakly tonight. The deluge of words, the hint of danger, put me on edge.

Ivy's Zippo sits on the table, too, next to my notepad. It gives me ideas. The chrome reflects some hidden side of me, but shoots it in another direction so I, the me on this side of the lighter, cannot see it. The chrome works like a mirror. My reflection is fortunate. It exists on the other side of Midnight.

The city closes in on us. I feel the weight of the mountains. I feel the cracks in the foundations, artificial tunnels and highway and apartments and malls, all underground waiting for the mountains to collapse. The ceiling crushes me. The waitress brings another drink. She knows I need it, but it's not enough.

I tell Ivy I need air. She waves me away. Have I already become merely that? I escape the poets and the liars, the vultures and the wolves. I reach the surface. Under the open night sky, under the constellations and a sickle moon, I swallow huge gulps of breath. Cars pass. People. Poets come and go. Around me, the prostitutes solicit their business, the cops patrol their streets, the card readers tell their futures. One of these is an old man, a blind man, though of course the blindness is a lie. It's part of the act. I play my part, pay my fee, and beg for a sign.

He pulls cards. He touches the faces of them, as if reading Braille. He mutters under his breath, he shakes his head, he touches the back of my hand. "There's a woman," he tells me.

I'm not impressed. "There's always a woman."

"I see you dancing," he says. "Or swinging in the wind. Hanging? That can't be right. Dancing, I'm sure of it. Twirling and...and..." He tapers off. He searches for the right word. He knows he's got me hooked, but he also knows I'll leave in thirty seconds if he doesn't find the word he needs. I have enough words. They bounce around in my head, a pinball machine gone amok and awry. He settles on, "Dancing."

"You said dancing."

He leans forward, gripping my wrist now. "I meant *dancing*. The kind with bullets."

I tell him I don't like guns.

"I know," he says.

"That doesn't prove anything," I remind him.

"I know that, too," he says. Then he spits out a title for me, something meant to prove himself: "*Poet*." He says it with venom. With teeth.

I like the way he says it. "Say that again."

"*Poet*," he whispers, but he's lost the vehemence and the weight. It's just a word now, meaning nothing it never meant before. "Dancer."

✳

●

I'm no dancer. I know a waltz from a tango, if I'm watching, because one has a rose and the other's set in Vienna. But I don't know a pirouette from an arabesque. I have no sense of balance. I like jazz when I don't have to think about it. Jazz should be felt. I don't have a dancer's body, either. I'm not lean or lithe, I'm not athletic, I'm not going to break or slide or twist.

Angeline wants to dance.

There's a place, she says, so we go. There's a lot of light, but it's inconsistent and frenetic. The numerous mirrors make me feel safe and exposed. The music is electric, heavy with bass, rhythmic but constant. It never eases up. It never breathes. One song flows into the next without any indication, as though the musicians cannot say anything unless other musicians say the same thing. As poetry, it fails. As jazz, it fails, except it steals liberally from jazz, and after a while I begin to think this is music I can like, this is music I can dance to.

I'm no dancer, except with Angeline. On the floor, pressed between other gyrating dancers, we express desire. We seek union. We tease and tempt. We touch and fade away. But every time I'm about to understand, every instance in which I start to think the moves make sense, that the fluidity transcends mere motion and emotion, the parameters change. Maybe it's the rhythm. Maybe it's the atmosphere. Maybe it's because I'm never any closer to breaking the mystery of dance than I ever was before.

"You dance like a madman," she tells me. So does she. We're soaked with sweat. We ache. We've unlocked things and hidden things. We have much to learn about each other.

I tell her, "I have a ring."

"That's not how you do it."

"I'm not doing it," I tell her. "I'm just giving you fair warning."

"I'll consider myself warned," she says.

We dance till dawn, and dance again in my living room, and bring the ways of dance to our lovemaking. I sleep for three days after.

●

Ivy fails to perform. Up on that stage, she reads with all the authority of a middle school boy caught masturbating in the girl's locker room. She makes eye contact with our feet. She sometimes looks up at me, but if she's seeking permission or adulation, I don't know and I don't offer either. They're not mine to give. She stumbles through the words, but the phraseology is there, the images striking. Only the lyricism is lacking, and that's entirely in her delivery.

Reluctantly, after arriving safely but uninspiringly at the end, she abandons the stage and takes the seat next to me. The waitress brings more whiskey. My notepad quivers in my hand.

She asks, "Where have you been?"

"Sleeping."

"You never tell me anything real," she says.

I shake my head. I throw out an "On the contrary" because I can. "Everything I've said has been real."

"But not what I want to hear."

Something's changed. I'm not yet sure what. "I thought you sought enlightenment."

She says, "Then enlighten me." Then she adds, "Or I'll find someone else who can."

I haven't really looked at her in a long time. She's always been a ghost to me, the misty remnants of something I and others like me have always feared we'd become. She's aimless, but not without destination. She looks sad, truly sad, in a way I've never seen before, and I wonder how long she's been this way.

"I can give you a lot more," I tell her.

"You can," she says. "But you don't."

Though our whiskey is empty, the waitress smartly avoids our little booth. Some kid is up there reading, or pretending to read. He's shier than Ivy ever was. He's got no potential.

"You want to know if you have potential," I say.

"We all *have* potential," she says.

"Ah." I shake my head. "Are you fulfilling yours?"

"Am I?"

I'm still shaking my head. "A question like that, the answer changes every day, every minute. On the stage just now, you strove for your potential with your words, but not with your voice."

"I see."

"You don't," I tell her. "You don't unleash yourself."

She leans closer to me, and I smell the perfume of her, perhaps the perfume she's always worn. She's so young. So eager. So very sad. Through gritted teeth, she says, "Unleash me."

*

I unleash her.

She's wild, uninhibited, risky and risqué, unafraid, uncontrollable. Ivy sheds more than her clothes when she undresses.

Her apartment is small. The bed, a chair, a table functioning as a desk, and a small shelf of books crowd the rooms. There's only one window, a sliver, that lets in no light. The walls absorb the lamp's feeble attempts at illumination. There's nothing here, real or not, except the poetess herself, and a bottle of bourbon-infused wine that, to me, tastes bitter, but I drink it when she offers.

"You don't know how long I've wanted to do that," she says.

"You're right," I say. "I don't."

She stares at me in the dark. I wonder what she sees. My scars? Ink tears slipping from the corner of my eye? She says nothing. She lies. She has much to say. It's up to me to breathe life into the conversation. Without it, we will wither. We will scatter. We will die.

I say, "You don't need me."

That's not what she expects.

I lay my palm on her chest, between her breasts. I apply only enough pressure. "You're fully armed. You're ready. All you need, you have within. Let it out."

"It's not that easy," she says.

"It can be."

She shakes her head. She unleashes me, rips open my scars, carves her name into my flesh with her fingernails, sucks the breath out of my mouth, gives me her own in exchange. It's urgent, and continues well past the time when we both should stop. Maybe outside it's dawn, or past dawn, or past dusk. There's no knowing. There's no caring.

After it's over, again, I whisper, "Write me a poem."

"I can't."

"Only one."

"I can't."

"I've already been writing one for you," I tell her.

"I've never seen it."

I shake my head. "You never will. It's not good. It's not deep poetry."

"Is it a love poem?"

I laugh. "No, of course not."

"Is it almost done?" she asks.

"I'm afraid so," I tell her, "but not yet. But this isn't about me. It's you. It's all you. Put pencil to paper. Tell the paper what you've been telling me all night."

"I've been lying to you."

"I don't care."

She gets her notepad, and her pen; and, in the dark, with full ferocity, she scrapes the paper. She's furious. She's intense. She's everything a poet should be. I leave her to it. I don't want to interfere. She's flipping pages and going at it even as I shut the door behind me.

The band plays.

I'm alone in a corner in the dark with my whiskey, my thoughts, and my notepad. I've got my own furious words to disgorge. It's a mess on the page, but I have light here, and music, and some semblance of solitude.

The singer recognizes me now. I've come one, two dozen times before, always with my notepad, sometimes with Ivy and sometimes with Angeline. Between sets, I almost see the face of the bassist, but even in silence the instrument overwhelms the player. The drummer plays with his sticks, pounding out a solo on the brick walls in the back corner. I can't hear it. The singer, the pixie blonde with vacuous words, buys me a shot of whiskey and sits across from me uninvited. In this world, especially in this city, we've transcended the need for invitations. We move in without regard to protocol or sensibility. It's not the world my mother fled when she took me here.

"You come, you listen, you scribble," she says. She smiles. She's pretty, with baby-soft cheeks and baby-fine blonde hair that probably shouldn't be as straight as she wants it. It curves, but doesn't curl. It wants to curl. She's inhibiting herself. "Have you nothing to say?"

"Often, I speak far too much," I tell her.

"You like the music?"

"Your drummer, he's got talent."

"The rest of us?"

I shrug. "I'm not a music critic."

"You must come back for a reason. Is it my voice?" She's smiling, flirting, but I don't know if I can lie to her.

"It's your eyes," I say.

"You can't see my eyes from here."

"Oh, but I can." I lean forward. I reach across the table and take her hands in mine. "Your eyes are hollow, just like your words. You may be pretending at depth, but you're swimming in the shallow end of the pool."

She doesn't pull her hands away. "That's cruel."

"I'm often cruel."

"I don't think that's true."

I'll give her a point for that. I give her a smile. "I'm often honest," I admit, "and that's usually the same thing."

"I have the feeling you know something I need to know," she tells me.

I have the same feeling, but I don't admit it.

"What's your name?" she asks.

"Smith," I say, pretending at suave. "Derek Smith."

"Call me Sage."

"That's not your name."

She squeezes my hands, releases them, stands. "I don't think you care about that."

After the break, the band plays again, the drummer keeping everyone in tempo, Sage making a sad attempt at guiding the audience through a forest of sorrow. She touches a real leaf here or there. She gives it more than I've seen her give before. She watches me from the stage. I don't ignore her, but I'm more involved with the pages in my notepad. I'm burning through them. I'm scratching out as much as I'm scribbling. The bass's rhythm overwrites my own. I'm taken by it, so the words I write are crap.

I tear out pages. I want to go back to the waitress. Sometimes, in the deep night, she'll bring me that extra shot of whiskey that keeps me going. I don't know how I've survived this long. I don't remember eating anything but Midnight's finest.

Since Sage is focused on me, she sings more coherently, more correctly, more evocatively. The man on the violin picks up on this. I don't think he misses a single note in the entire set. The drummer is their glue. The bass threatens to swallow the stage. Before it's over, I have to argue for another drink. The bar closes. I hate when a bar closes.

"Let's go for a walk," Sage tells me.

"Through the streets?"

"Through the park."

We're not far from the Mirage. It's all impossible trees and ravens and winding paths and madmen proclaiming the end times. We walk, we hold hands, we trade stories about orange juice and wild cherries and surfboards.

"What is it you think I know?" I ask her.

She giggles. She giggles a lot. She doesn't trust herself to form the words, doesn't trust her mouth to say them, doesn't trust me or anyone else to hear what she means. I can't help her work through her issues. Instead of answering, she lies. "I don't know."

Later, sitting by a fountain, she asks me to tell her a poem, to read something from my notepad. It contains nothing complete, nothing near ready. She convinces me anyhow. I read broken fragments, orphans, miserable rhymes. For the first time since I've ever known her, she doesn't look sad.

I should be frightened. I'm not smart enough for that.

When I'm done, she kisses me. Embarrassed, she apologizes, then runs off into the forest like a pixie.

A crow, my father, laughs at me.

She wears a shade of indigo reminiscent of the middle of the night, and since it's always the middle of the night here I'm certain it's meant to be camouflage. It doesn't work, though, when you have a face that demands attention, when your hair cascades over your shoulders like thousand-foot tall waterfalls in China. She sits at a table, alone again, in a restaurant, and I'm sure I've seen her there before.

I take the seat across from her before the wait staff can arrive with water. She looks at me with eyes like weapons and says, "Do I know you?"

"Unambivalently, yes." She's still a mystery. I've learned nothing of her.

When she smiles, it's like the world's cracking open and I'm only just learning to take my first step. I teeter over precipices filled with pools of acidic ink. I reach down, hold my hands close to the liquid surface, feel the bubbling, boiling, roiling power.

She pulls her hand away.

I don't think I ever saw her before this place, but it wasn't tonight. It runs together. She's an ocean sunrise in disguise.

"You've asked me questions," I tell her.

"I have."

"You've challenged me," I tell her.

"I have."

"I like to be challenged."

She doesn't respond to this. She should say, "I know," but she's skipped, and it throws off my rhythm. I have to catch my breath to regain my equilibrium.

"I like to be challenged," I say again. "I do." There, that's better. "You've also threatened me."

She raises her eyebrows. "Have I?"

"Everything about me has changed. I see things I've never seen before. I hear what's always gone unheard. I'm learning things."

"What are you learning?"

I shake my head. She's throwing my rhythm again. "Now is not the time for questions. This is my soliloquy."

"You get one of those?" she asks.

"Of course I do. We all get at least one. Two, if we're fortunate. For the greatest of us, people like Shakespeare, like Poe, an unlimited abundance of them await at arm's length, free and ready for the plucking." I lower my voice, confiding. "Many among these great, however, are unnamed and anonymous, devoured by history so that no trace remains."

"That's awful."

"Yes," I admit. "It is."

Men who are not as well dressed as they should be considering their positions arrive to inquire about our wants and desires. They bring glasses of water and folded menus and listen to every requested nuance—no tomatoes, for instance.

"Go on," Angeline says. "Your soliloquy."

"Ah, that." I smile, because it's all I can do. I see the ocean sunrise underneath, I see the lines of her lips and the dimples at the small of her back. I see the wasted words and crumpled papers wherein I tried to create something that matched the beauty of her, the elegance of her, the grace and the perfection. Sometimes, I must eventually realize but have yet to admit, there simply are no words. "I'm learning things. I'm growing. I'm dying inside, and being rebirthed, and running around in circles. I'm catching all the things I've never caught before, and throwing back all the things I've always grasped. I'm turning things over. I'm exploring."

"I think," she says, interrupting again, "you've always been something of an explorer." I'm glad of the interruption. I have no idea what I'm saying. I'm rambling.

Food arrives. A violinist strolls between tables. It's not the guy from the band. This one is skilled, albeit somewhat stilted. He's played these songs so often, he's lost the passion for them. When he comes near, I wave him over, I can wave a person over these days, and I tell him, "Play me something you've never played before."

He's confused, so I ease his suffering with generous, surreptitious compensation, and tell him as plainly as I can, "Invent something."

"Something romantic?" he asks.

I shrug. "If that's how you feel."

He does an admirable job of it. He plays notes he hasn't heard in years, puts them together nicely.

There's nothing perfect about the tune; it strays, it hiccups, it meanders. But it's emotive. It's provocative. Though it's a sad song, it makes me happy. And it makes Angeline happy.

"Is this my song?" she asks.

"I can't imagine why not."

"I think it's wonderful," she says.

"You think a great many things are wonderful," I remind her.

Then I throw the questions at her, easy first, until I can get through to the most difficult question ever asked. "Am I wonderful?"

"Yes," she says, with enthusiasm.

"How long has it been?"

"Three months, a year, perhaps a decade," she says. She shrugs. "I don't think I care."

"Neither do I. How much longer can it possibly be?"

She narrows her eyes and throws a question back at me. "What makes you think it will go beyond this table, this night, this sonata?"

I waste a moment's thought on the violinist. How much time did I buy?

I show Angeline my mother's ring, the one with the diamond. I'm on one knee. I'm doing everything traditionally. The whole restaurant seems to notice. Except for the violin, all other sounds and noises fade away. "Ah, but I think we might very well have a long, long time ahead of us."

She smiles. She takes the ring, slips it on precisely the right finger, per tradition, and says, "I think you're right."

The man from the shadows, Robin, Rob if you prefer, waits again in the shadows. He finds me at random on a street under the eternal night. He steps out nonchalantly, marveling at the faux-coincidence of our meeting at precisely the spot where he's been waiting for me. I've never had a stalker before, not one who wanted me dead.

He does, too. I'm sure of it. There's a knife tucked into his jeans, a butterfly knife; he can make it spin and sing and dance, he can dazzle, he can cut and carve and lunge and slice.

I start. I don't need to begin with his lies. "I've been expecting you."

"You have?"

"Since you started your thievery, I've been conscious of every word. I expect hands to lunge out of the walls and steal the letters, the phrases, the thoughts and ideas. I share my notepad out of desperation, to ascertain the current existence of ugly things I've written before. I expect the pages to be blank, but thus far they haven't been. That can only mean one thing."

He tilts his head. He grins. He doesn't mind being caught; he wants the challenge. He expects nothing less of me. He asks, "What's that?"

"You haven't gotten to me yet."

"Wouldn't you know?"

My initial impression proves unfounded. "I thought you might be a bit sneakier."

"There's no need for stealth," he says. "I can come out and say everything I want to say."

"To this point," I remind him, "you haven't."

He shoves his hands in his coat pockets. He's fingering that knife, stroking it, exciting it. The weapon wants to play. It practically pulses in his coat. I'm surprised he can stand it.

On a nearby mailbox, the crow, my father, alights. Curiously, he merely watches. And preens. Damn crows.

"Okay, you've got me there," Rob says. "I haven't said anything. But I've been meaning to. Building up the nerve, you might say."

"Please," I say, "get it over with."

"You stole my girl."

It's laughable, so I laugh. What else should I do? I consider my options. He's got a knife, but so do I. I've also got a pen, a notepad, an extensive knowledge of words like *conundrum* and *palindrome* and *conflagration*, none of which are presently useful. I can run, or walk, or turn my back, with the ease of a panther.

He says, "It's not funny."

"Actually," I admit, "I have no idea what you're talking about. I've never stolen anything in my life, and I have no girls to speak of."

"Oh, I've been watching you."

I nod. I know this.

"You've got at least a dozen, maybe two, hanging on your every word. You trade on your past."

"I don't remember my past."

"Shall I remind you?"

I consider it, but it's tangential. "No," I say. "Go on. Who's your *girl?*" I don't like the way he uses the word, so I spit it back with some venom, but thus far I'm not following him. I need a name. Any name. Give me a name, and maybe I can put it together with one of the half-sketched poems in my notepad. Maybe I can recall a face, the words we shared, the touch of her lips.

He gives me a name.

I don't hear him. Maybe it's a bit of thunder, distant, rolling through at precisely the moment he speaks. Maybe a subway rumbled to a halt beneath the street. Maybe I simply don't want to hear it. But I feel I owe him something, an answer to the accusation if nothing else, and I cannot properly respond without knowing. "I'm sorry," I say, "I did not hear that."

He enunciates carefully, exaggeratedly, letting every syllable slide from his tongue as if a whole word in itself. It's condescending. I have to concentrate to put the syllables together. He says it with an unusual, imperfect accent, another thing he's stolen. He says, "Anne. Jeh. Lean."

I smile. I call him a liar.

✳

There are two kinds of people in the world. There are always two. No one who describes kinds of people can break it down more cleanly than that, but they're always wrong. There's no such thing as black and white anymore. This twenty-first century doesn't allow it. Different shades, hues, tones, tints, and dyes paint uncertainty over any imaginable two-kinds system. In fact, there are people who know what's going on, and people who don't know. In the middle, there are the people who know only a particular thing, or know that thing from a particular vantage point. I don't know what I mean, precisely, except to say that I completely and utterly understand Robin, Rob if you prefer, despite that he makes no sense.

"Theft," I tell Angeline, "has certain requirements. I fail to see how I've met any of those requirements."

She smiles. She shrugs. She doesn't care. She says, "You didn't steal me." My mother's ring shines on her finger like it belongs there.

I can't shake the feeling that, perhaps, I did steal. "I swept you away from somewhere."

"Oh, yes, absolutely," she admits. "Monotony. Boredom. Listlessness."

"Are you describing this man Robin?" I ask.

"Not intentionally," she says, "but yes."

"The restaurant?"

"It's a special place for us," she says. "He wasn't there."

"Was he supposed to be?"

She thinks on this. There are multiple answers. On some level, any of them could be correct. She says, "No. You were supposed to be."

"*I was.*"

"He wasn't."

"Thievery implies conditions," I tell her again. "A right to ownership."

"No one has ever owned me."

I'm puzzled. "Have I not staked my own claim?"

She holds up her hand, putting my mother's ring between us. She asks, "This?" She answers, "This is no claim, Derek, but a promise. Are you telling me you don't understand?"

"Oh, no, I understand," I say.

"What have you promised?"

"To obey," I say, "and be obeyed."

"There is no past," she says. "There is no shadow in the dark, unless we ourselves are the shadows. You told me that, I believe."

"I may have said something to that effect."

"Obey me now," she says. "Make me scream."

✸

Some weapons do more damage than others. I don't like guns. Too loud, too messy, too uncontrollable. Sure, I've got a friend who can hit the eraser on a pencil in your hands from three hundred yards away with a 9mm, but that's a special talent and I won't be putting that to the test again anytime soon. Knives are also messy, but personal. You have to get close, breathe the same air, feel the knots of your opponent's muscles. Poison has a certain elegance, but the waitress bringing me my poison cannot be bought. She knows the heart and soul of me. She could kill me more easily with her eyes.

I killed a man once. I used the right weapon. I can't trust Robin, Rob if you prefer, to be so meticulous.

Evan poeticizes on stage. Ivy rests her head in her hands and sighs. I scribble in my notepad, but all my words are violent. I loathe them. I go through several pages, but I cannot completely tune Evan out. His words leak onto my paper. The juxtaposition of his perfect inflections and my vicious meanderings could, potentially, with a little finesse, result in unheralded beauty. Instead, I get babies and strained peas.

At some point, I lay down my pen, I close my eyes, I simply listen. I hear Evan's words as he finishes. I hear Ivy's breath. I hear the waitress bring more whiskey. She touches my shoulder as she walks away, whispers in my ear, implores me to take care of myself.

Silence follows Evan because no one's brave enough to climb that stage. The stool sits empty, no longer inviting but challenging would-be poets to rise to the occasion. The spotlight falls flatly against the wall, a metaphor of something I can no longer recall.

Ivy says, "I found a new teacher."

"You're finally done with me?" I ask.

"You finished first." In fact, I didn't, but that's not what she means. "You promised to teach me the things I need."

"I promised nothing," I remind her.

"You implied it."

"I've always answered your questions," I tell her. "I've given you all the things you've asked for. What is it you want?"

"He's taught me things about meter I didn't think I could know. He's revealed rhymes I never imagined. He's connected disparate concepts in ways that, frankly, would make you jealous."

"I'm not the jealous type," I tell her.

"I know."

"Then why are you here?"

"Can I not have two teachers?"

"No."

"Why not? I need more than you can give me."

"Then you've taken all you can take from me. There's nothing left."

"That's not true."

"Of course it's true," I say. "That's why you're telling me."

"He admires you."

"A lot of people have claimed to," I admit.

"He says I shouldn't leave you."

"Then don't."

"He says you still have lessons to be taught."

Her phrasing is wrong. I can't ignore that. I open my eyes, hold her head with one hand behind her neck, draw her close enough that we can share a secret. I touch her ear with my lips as I ask in a whisper, "What does he intend to teach me?" I don't let go. I wait. I wait a long time. I can feel her lips trembling against the side of my throat. She cries silently. The cold tears slide down her cheek and fall onto my neck. I let go of the tension and hold her, simply hold her, and allow her the luxury of crying for me in secret.

✸

O

When the band plays, they play for me. The players don't know this. The faceless nameless bass player slips inside the instrument and gives everything away except identity. That's all that's lacking: that one thing that separates you from all the others like you. I cross my fingers in some sign of unity, respect, and hopefulness. A day may come where the player steps out of that shadow.

The drummer, as always, holds them together. He guides them and sets them off in random directions. They're more jazz today, more impromptu, more enlivened. He doesn't just permit this, he encourages it. He follows along, pushing and prompting, leading from behind, providing context and purpose.

The violinist misses his notes, but he catches the tone, so it's okay.

And Sage, singing there, wonderful and beautiful and haunting, is slipping further into the hollowness that's followed her here. She doesn't belong in Midnight. This City of Night will consume her. This City of Night will eviscerate her. This City of Night will disintegrate her by degrees, first making fine dust and sand of her insides, then fusing them into smooth, fragile glass. When her heart succumbs, when it's solid and dangerous to herself and to others, it will shatter. The shards will protrude from her chest and her back, and will fill the hollowness of her eyes with sharp, icy death.

I feel responsible.

The more she feels, the deeper she gets into anything whatsoever, the closer she comes to this end.

Between sets she sits with me, she tells me stories about her childhood, the beaches, the sands, the gothic tendencies, the exotic dancing that paid her way through college.

"You were a dancer?" I ask.

She narrows her eyes. "I don't dance like that anymore."

"But you do dance." It's not a question.

"Not when I sing."

"Of course not."

"That would be foolish," she says. "And arrogant."

I ask if she's ever been to the rooftops, if she's ever danced under the light of the full moon, to the beats of only our hearts.

She says, "Tonight."

But she means in the morning, in the darkest hours before dawn. Even in this Midnight, even where the sun never shows its skin, darkness comes in degrees. The music never ends. You hold it inside yourself. You bring it with you. So we dance, slow and close, two bodies melded together, under the soft light of the moon.

"I'm broken," she tells me.

"All of us are."

"Me more than others."

"You're not broken," I tell her. "You're lost." Her eyes reflect this, but she looks away. "You're away from home."

"I have my music."

I shake my head. "You restrain yourself."

"Are you saying I shouldn't?"

"I'm saying you shouldn't."

She smiles, lays her pixie head against my chest. "You think you know so much. Why haven't you fixed yourself?"

"I'm not imperfectly broken," I tell her.

"And you think I am?"

"You think you're not?"

"You're right," Sage says. "I've lost myself here. But sometimes I think, and only sometimes, maybe I can find where I belong."

"This is Midnight," I say. "Nobody leaves."

"Maybe where I belong," Sage says, "isn't a place, but a person."

I warn her, "That's excessively romantic."

She kisses me, gingerly, on the lips. She uses one of those weighty, meaningful whispers, and says, "Maybe it's you."

This is one of those moments that can reverberate through the history of you. When you're old and feeble and looking back, this is a moment, no matter what happens next, that will always leave you wondering. What if it went some other way? What if the things that happened didn't?

The crow, my father, shakes his head and flies away.

"You've got the soul of a poet," Sage tells me. "You belong here, this City of Night. It suits you. You and the city breathe together. You can help me, I'm sure of it."

"You're desperate," I tell her.

"Damn right, I am."

I close my eyes. We've stopped dancing; we stand there, in each other's arms, trembling, inhaling and exhaling in opposition to the other. She kisses me again, all softness and tenderness. She holds back her desperation. She holds back her desire. She's willing to let her audience take, but she's not yet able to give.

I have her face in my hands. I hold her away from me. If she casts her hollow eyes upon mine, if she looks at me straightly and steadily, I might forget the things I've forgotten. I tell her I think I know a way to help her. Sage moves gently, and so do I. All urgency is held back. There's no rush. We slip in and out of each other quietly, like the whisperings of ghosts, like the barest traces of shadow.

Before I leave her, there on the rooftops with only my father and his kind to watch over her, I whisper a heavy promise.

✳

She says she loves me. I believe her.

O

The sign says Midnight Psychiatric Institution. Most people just call it The Asylum. Some who know better call it Midnight Tears. There's a rumor the place has been closed for years, but it's not true. The chains outside have rusted over the gate, but they're no less strong. I sneak in the same way I always do. I slip through the glassless window, I climb the stairs, I smile at the nurses and orderlies and doctors in their white coats. Sometimes, I think they think I live here.

My mother's chamber is large and empty. I can imagine myself chained to the cement floor, half naked, sweaty and crying, staring into the faces of anonymous visitors.

The crack where my mother's ring had fallen has spread its tendrils throughout the asylum. There are cracks in the walls, outside and in, wood or stone. There are cracks in the mirrors, all save one, but one is all I will need.

I whisper, "Mom?" No one answers. No one comes to tell me where she's gone. The floor in her chamber is a network of webbed cracks; if I walk too heavily, it will break and I will fall. Who knows what madness awaits beneath?

One of the nurses looks familiar. I ask her, "Where's my mom?"

She checks a chart. She almost ignores me entirely. "You'll have to ask the doctors."

"I can't talk to the doctors again."

"Afraid they'll commit you?" she asks.

"What did you do to my mother?"

The nurse lowers her chart and meets my stare. "What did *I* do?" she asks. "You drove her mad, Mr. Smith. You drove her here. You *took* her here, told the doctors to keep her until she died, and then you visited and visited and visited until you got everything you wanted from her."

"I only wanted her to be my mom."

"You took her applause and her love, her talent, and her words. You took her *ring.*"

"She gave it."

The nurse sneers. "She gave you everything, didn't she?"

"You're wasting your time," the crow, my father says from the windowsill.

The nurse takes her charts and goes away. She leaves me with that sneer. It hurts. I sit on the floor, where I would've been chained, where I would've cried, and I wipe tears from my eyes before they can form.

"You've accomplished nothing," the crow, my father says.

"I've found..." But I cannot find the words.

"You're not a poet. You're not even alive."

"Ah, but I am alive." I stand up to the crow, my father. I raise my head and I raise my voice. "Why must you haunt me?"

"We *are* connected by blood, Derek."

"We're divided by our cities."

"You're pathetic," the crow, my father tells me.

"You think your fate is tied to the fate of this city. It's not. This city will be grand, and it will be terrible. It will save millions and destroy millions. Five hundred years from now, this city will persist, but there'll be no memory of you, there'll be nothing of you at all but your mother's work. You were the least of her accomplishments."

"You're wrong."

"You keep saying so. Prove it."

I yell. I swing at my father though I cannot possibly reach the crow on the windowsill. Isn't that the way a boy becomes a man: challenge your father? Have I been nothing but a boy all these decades? I rage at the sill. I ignore the nurses and the orderlies, the patients and the doctors. They leave me alone in this chamber, my mother's chamber, where nothing remains of her but the cracks in the floor.

I hurl words at the sill. I sling the best and the worst I've got. I unleash. It takes a long while to spend myself. I collapse to my knees again, I hold out my arms as if chained, and sob.

The nurse brings me water and a cookie. She holds me from behind and says soothing nonsensical things. She tells me, "You couldn't leave while she was here. You're free now, Mr. Smith. You're free."

"I need sedation," I tell her.

She shakes her head. "Not without talking to the doctors."

"I won't talk to the doctors again."

The nurse is evil. "Then find your own sedation."

✳

O

Evan says things. His words vibrate and resonate and leave impressions. The waitress brings fresh whiskey. Ivy sighs. Ivy sighs again.

"You want me to say something," I say, which might count as something but not here, not now.

"You've been crying."

"Of course I've been crying."

"Talk to me."

"What would you have me say?"

"Tell me something truthful."

I shake my head. "I'll tell you something honest."

"You've always been honest with me."

"Mostly," I admit.

"It's my turn."

"Is it?"

"It's time for a lesson."

I glance at the stage. Evan's words bounce off the walls. They can crush, or they can be severed. He doesn't care which. That's his secret.

But Ivy shakes her head. "I wish it was him," she says. "I would learn anything from him."

"Have you not been listening?" I ask.

"Outside," Ivy says. "Upstairs. On the rooftops."

Again on the rooftops. The different roofs are all the same. There's gravel, or paved paths, industrial sized air conditioning units, pipes and vents and wires and antennae. A cold wind whips through us. Ivy lights a cigarette with her Zippo lighter, inhales deeply, then throws the cigarette aside. "I've had enough," she says.

"It was never more than a crutch."

"I'm no longer hobbled."

I raise an eyebrow. I can do that. "No?"

She hands me her chrome Zippo, pulls out a piece of paper, and reads me her newest poem. It's gorgeous, but it's sentimental. It's raw and rough and honest, and it's about me. It's about love and hatred and fear. It's only about three minutes long, but it's piercing. She reads it better than she's read anything before. She asks, "What do you think?"

"I think it's beautiful."

"I think it's awful," she says, "that I don't feel that way anymore."

"No?"

"You don't touch me," she says. "Not like you did."

"You've grown."

"I've outgrown you," she says.

"Oh." I have no response.

"She'll learn much more from me," he says.

He appears out of nowhere, as though formed of wind and ice and shadow. He reaches for Ivy's hand, but his eyes are on me and only me. Robin, Rob if you prefer, grins at me and says, "You're nothing."

"I've heard that before," I tell him. Indeed, the crow, my father, watches us now from the very edge of the rooftop. We're a dozen stories high.

"You've lost," he says. "You'll lose everything."

"I didn't realize it was a contest."

"It's always been a contest," Ivy tells me, but I don't look at her. She's not the one here to kill me.

"I expected worse," I admit.

"We're not done," he says. He turns to Ivy, drops to a knee. "I'm yours, Ivy. Will you be mine? Will you marry me? Will you stay with me forever, fight alongside me in my wars as I fight alongside you in yours?"

"You think poetry is war?" I ask.

"Yes," Ivy says, to both of us. "Yes, yes, a thousand times yes."

My mother's ring is already on her finger. He puts his hand over it. He looks at me through the corner of his eyes. "We'll always be tied together," he says. Then to me, and only me, he says, "I have stolen everything from you, don't you see? You can die now." He nods toward the edge, toward the crow, my father. "You're free to jump now."

I look at my father. He says nothing. He flies away. He abandons me. I walk to the edge of the rooftop and look down at the pulsing, brilliantly lit City of Night, at the streets and the mouths of tunnels and the windows in the mountainside, at the gardens and the monuments, buildings old and new, at this twisting metaphor of my own inaccessible life.

Rob whispers encouragement. When I look back, Ivy has turned away. The wind catches her hair. She's never been so beautiful, or so poisonous.

Rob has a gun, a black steel Oliveri. He holds it at his hip like a crime noir gangster. It's pointed at me. "This only ends one way," he tells me.

"I expected better from you," I say, and I jump.

O

You expect the last flight of your life to end quickly and sharply. But it doesn't end that way at all. The crow, my father, had flown away over a line of fire escapes. It rocks and rings when I hit it, and it bites into my ankles and calves and back, but nothing breaks—nothing except the window when I kick it. I glance up before going inside, and there's Robin, Rob if you prefer, staring over the edge, his mouth an O, the gun hanging limply in his hand. I give him a little grin and a wave.

It's not a goodbye wave. It's one of beckoning.

He's committed now. He has to follow.

The woman's apartment is messy. I come in through the kitchen. She sits in the living room watching something bland on the television box. She glances at me with some degree of fear and a bit of hope. Maybe I'm here to relieve the monotony? Maybe I can save her?

I'll save someone, maybe, but not her.

I say, "Thank you," though she knows not why, and burst into a dim, dank hall. There are other apartment doors, perhaps a closet, a set of stairs going down, and a frightening elevator. Once, I dreamt of elevators crashing, and I've never boarded one since. I'm not about to change that.

There are other stairs. It takes half a minute, way too long, to find them, despite that I've been here before, and climb them again. When I break out into the open air, Ivy sways at the edge, staring down, quivering, crying, looking beautiful and, in her head, composing what she thinks will be the poetry of her life.

She turns as I grab her arm. "Oh, God," she says. She falls into me, violently shaking her head.

Rob explodes onto the rooftop with his finger on the trigger. He shoots. I'll never forget the echo of the gunshot. The force of the bullet nearly knocks me off my feet; but it's not me that it hits. It's all I can do to keep Ivy from plummeting over the edge. Her blood burns me like acid.

Rob's face is an expressionist painting of fury. He raises the gun again.

A murder of crows rise up from all sides. The flurry of black wings, of angry caws, of beaks that pick at dead flesh, confuses and disorients everyone but me. I knew my father would never abandon me. He never has.

Rob rushes blindly forward. I'm not so blind. I let Ivy drop to the rooftop, not over the edge, and rise to meet him. For a moment, it seems we'll both fall over the edge. The gun escapes. The wind gales. Rob screams. I scream. We all scream as the world rages. We struggle like wrestlers, like bears, right there at the edge, neither strong enough to throw over the other. I want to be that strong. I want to be that swift, that courageous, that skilled. I'm none of these things. I'm merely fighting for my life. Again.

In the end, I cannot save myself.

A gunshot settles it. Rob looks surprised. I'm surprised. His expressionist painting of a face has distorted into something more closely resembling pain. His grip on me slackens. He slips to the side, closer to the edge, and teeters. He won't fall without my help. Ivy, on her back, bleeding, crying, had only strength enough for one shot.

I extricate myself from Rob's grasp. I let go. I think about giving the tiniest little shove. I can watch Rob tumble over the side of the building, turning end over end until crashing into the ground. Though I may be a thief, I am no murderer. I step back and let him drop to his knees. I recognize the position.

Ivy says, "He lied to me."

I look at her. I cannot quite smile, but I give her something. "I know."

O

I sleep and dream for days. My dreams are chaotic messes of flying and running and splintered glass. I finish all the whiskey in the apartment and stare out the window as the storm encroaches. When storm comes to Midnight, it comes to stay. It crackles and releases deluge after deluge. Waterfalls form off the sides of buildings. There's one outside my window. I could descend it in a canoe. Maybe it will take me elsewhere.

I have no phone. It doesn't ring. I don't miss it. I don't need the contact. I need to work through the visions, the images, and the words. Yes, when I wake, I scribble in my notepad, I cross out whole lines and tear out pages. I burn through an entire pad and several pens. I have plenty.

The words I write aren't worthy of poetry; the notepad serves as a scratchpad, a sketchbook, a collection of raw and rough and honest ideas rather than fully formed verse. I whisper secrets to my mother; she must, somewhere, be listening, lying beneath the surface of a pool of ink, eyes open but clouded, lips parted and cold. The crow, my father, makes no appearance.

When I use up this pad, I scratch out words on the walls, into the coffee table, the posts of my bed.

When I use up the pens, I cry and collect the ink tears in an antique perfume bottle. Indigo swims inside the glass like eels. I remember swimming in the ocean. I remember ocean sunrises and the middle of the night and a dress once worn by a woman I will never forget.

She comes at dawn or dusk—I cannot be sure. She makes me drink water, but she's also brought whiskey. She feeds me bread and cheese and chocolate. She holds me like a baby. She wears my mother's ring on precisely the right finger. I touch the back of her hand, her fingernails, her lips. She smiles and repeats promises already made.

"You decide when," I remind her.

She smiles. She brushes back my hair and wipes my brow with a washrag. She says, "Now. Today. Today would be perfect."

She wants a preacher, a priest, a rabbi, anyone with authority. A captain would be good, but there's no shore at Midnight and therefore no ships, no pirates, no mates, and no captains. There's a man called the Admiral, but I don't believe he ever served. He's old and, quite honestly, a bit off the tune. When he roams the Midnight Tears, he does so with pride and honor. But he doesn't see who he's talking to anymore.

"Not the court," Angeline says. "Not the court alone."

"Of course not."

"That would be...less than what we should have."

On the streets, there's a reverend who wanders, a man dressed all in black who will tell you he is no priest. He has a daughter. He sees things I cannot. He points them out to me, sometimes, when he's on the corner, on his milk crate, spouting words like poetry in every language imaginable. He's a madman, if ever there's been one, but he's outside, on the streets, and today, at my corner.

"Yes," Angeline says, giving the Wandering Reverend her biggest smile, "he would do nicely."

"Would I?" he asks.

"We want to be wedded," I tell him. "We want to be wedded now, today, in the eyes of a god."

"Don't you care which god?" he asks.

I don't. Angeline doesn't, either, so we don't answer.

"That's a beautiful ring," he says of my mother's ring on Angeline's finger.

"It's old," I tell him.

"It's a real promise," he says. "It's binding, more so than anything I can say or hold you to. Do you understand that?"

"I do."

"Save the *I do* for the proper moment," he says, turning to Angeline. "You know what you're getting into?"

"It's up to me, is it not?" she asks.

"You know who he is and what he is and all the things he'll give you, now and forever?" the Wandering Reverend asks.

"I do."

"Now's not the moment," the Wandering Reverend says, "but I suppose it's done, then, is it not? You do, you both do, so hold each other's hands, here before me, and answer me these questions." He asks. They're quite traditional, and quite natural in his voice. He could be a power. He is a power. I hadn't feared him before today. "Do you, Derek Smith?" he asks, and "Do you, Angeline?" We both respond with the proper words. We have witnesses there on the street, salespeople and executives and bakers and bankers, taxi drivers, prostitutes, beggars and thieves, and poets. Yes, the poets pour onto the streets for our impromptu wedding, even Ivy, who silently cries.

When the Wandering Reverend says, "You may kiss the bride," I do so enthusiastically, and the crowd roars its approval.

✳

O

"I suppose I have other lessons to learn," Ivy says. She pushes the whiskey away from her. "I cannot believe you still sit with me."

"You still have lessons," I say.

"You're not who you were."

"Neither are you."

"I've grown."

"So you said. But still, you're here."

"Other lessons," she admits.

"Then we should begin."

The waitress brings fresh whiskey, but we've barely touched what she's already brought. The line of empty glasses is not so impenetrable as it's been. "Is everything okay?" she asks me.

"Everything will be," I tell her.

"I've always known that," the waitress tells me, patting my shoulder as she goes. I catch her hand and pull her, gently, closer.

I whisper so that no one, not even Ivy, can hear. "You lie."

"So what if I do?"

"You were concerned."

"I was always concerned," she tells me.

I smile. "I like that."

"Don't get used to it." She walks away. I won't see her again tonight.

Evan's up on the stage, screaming words now, scratchy and rough words that aren't near as clever as I once believed. Even Ivy ignores him. She scribbles in her notepad. I scribble in mine. She bites her lower lip as she writes, just as I do. She picked it up from me. She's never been more beautiful.

I set down my pen. I look into Ivy's eyes. I ask, "*Is* everything alright?"

She smiles at me but doesn't slow down her scribbling. She says, "It will be."

O

Sage sings with fragile melancholy, but it's lost all its edge. She sways like a pixie, not like a dancer. She thinks she sings for me, but she doesn't sing for anyone anymore.

"She's still wonderful," Angeline tells me. I agree.

The violinist hits his notes. It's nice to hear. He hits most of his notes, anyhow, and that's probably good enough, at least for the moment. He's exploring. He's expanding. He's learning his limitations but also breaking through them.

"He hasn't found himself yet," Angeline suggests. "He hasn't got the emotion." I agree. Sage has got the emotion, but she masks it. She battles it.

The bass absorbs its player. For some, there's no hope. Perhaps the player should turn to photography, or the culinary arts. We can always use another good chef. This city is in painfully short supply. The player may have talent with oils or with knives, but there's no coming out from behind that instrument.

Angeline agrees.

There's no drummer tonight. Maybe he's sick. Maybe he's dead. Maybe he's just not strong enough to hold together a broken band.

Angeline doesn't mention the drummer. As the band reaches the end of its last set, she leans over and kisses my neck and says into my ear, "I'll be waiting for you."

She's gone before Sage reaches the table. Sage sits. Sage pouts. "I saw you," she says.

"I heard you," I tell her.

"We're doomed," Sage says.

I take her hand. "No," I tell her. "The band is doomed. For you, though, I believe we may find salvation."

"I cannot have the things I want."

"No one can have all the things they want."

"You're cold to me now," she says.

"On the contrary," I say, "I've never felt more deeply, more passionately, about anything."

"Not even her?"

"Forget her. This isn't about her. It's about you."

"Me and you?"

I shake my head. "I have something to show you."

The Midnight Tears lays hidden in a rundown, abandoned, industrial area, where there are crows and shadows and people in the shadows whom you do not want to meet. They stir in the presence of a blonde little pixie like Sage, but I don't let her linger. I bring her to the gate where the rusted chains hold it closed.

"My mother died in there," I tell her.

"No."

"Yes."

"Why bring me here, then?" she asks.

"There's still hope," I tell her.

I lead her through the iron fence and in through a glassless window. We avoid the orderlies and the doctors, though the nurse that sees us acknowledges me with a sad smile and a weak nod. The cracks have grown worse. They're out of control. They've infected the nurse's flesh. Everything here is so fragile, I'm afraid.

We climb the stairs, we pass other patients. The place has never been so quiet or hollow. I lead Sage by the hand; her grip is tight. She trembles.

"I don't believe in hope," she says. "Not in a place like this. A place like this, there's never been hope, there's never been comfort or justice. Why would you bring me here?"

"I'm not bringing you *here*," I tell her.

She stops walking. She makes me stop. I hope she knows I'm doing this for her. "You love me," she says.

"Of course I do."

"Are you lying to me?"

"Of course not," I say. "You don't understand love, if you think that I can. But I will tell you this, if it helps. You *will* understand, one day, perhaps when you're older or, perhaps, when you find that place you're looking for."

"You think you know things," she says. "I think you make things up."

"I think you're right," I say. "But you're also wrong."

The one mirror is still intact. The cracks have circled it without penetrating. It's full length, in my mother's chamber, where I can still see her sitting on her wooden stool and I can still see me chained to the concrete floor. Now, it's desolate and stark.

We look at ourselves in the mirror. It's smudged and dirty and very, very old, so the image is glossy and distorted. Except for Sage's blonde hair, the mirror knows nothing of vibrancy. It's a long mirror. It looks deeply into us, just as we look deeply into it. There are greater and lesser paths, perhaps, and maybe I have no idea where it really leads. Maybe I only think I know.

"You're willing to lose me?" Sage asks.

"You were never mine to lose."

"I'm not ready," she says.

"You'll wither here," I tell her. "You'll die. You need the sun, but you also need the loss."

"The loss of you?" she asks.

I nod. "And the loss of who you've been."

"Who, exactly, have I been?" she asks.

I admit I don't know. "But you'll find out."

The mirror shimmers. The cracks have thickened, and the mirror shifts.

"Come with me," Sage says.

I let go of her hand. I've already found my place, here in this dismal City of Night; I belong with an ocean sunrise and the indigo of midnight.

Sage steps across the mirror's threshold.

She shimmers on the other side. She turns, puts her hand up to the glass. She's wearing my mother's ring on precisely the right finger. She says, "I love you."

I touch the glass, but cannot take her hand, not anymore. I whisper, because whispers carry strength no shout can ever know. "I love you."

She turns and walks through the gloom into something else. I can only imagine what else.

O

Evan recites his mediocre poetry. He looks to me for approval, but I cannot give it. Half the poets have disappeared or wandered off or simply never returned. I don't recognize the place.

The waitress brings me whiskey. I sip. It tastes bitter, like it's lost all its vibrancy and all its depth. I have my notepad. I look to it for my own salvation. Finally, finally, after all of this and everything, I write a poem worth writing. I reread it. I cry. I take out Ivy's Zippo and set fire to the page. It burns perfectly. Beautifully. Completely.

ACKNOWLEDGMENTS

This novella wouldn't exist as a standalone book like this if not for Brett Tiano of 7 Story Rabbit. He wanted to make the audiobook. I narrate. You should go find it.

Originally, this novella was part of *Tales of the Fantastic and the Phantasmagoric*, so I must thank Edgar Allan Poe for his amazing influence on a much younger me.

As always, a special thanks to Sabine and the Rose Fairy. You will always be with me.

ABOUT THE PROJECT AND AUTHOR

John Urbancik's business card says he's a Writer, Photographer, and Adventurer, though it could just as easily have claimed Madmen, Poet, and Thief.

In addition to books of poetry and photography, and a nonfiction book based on the 100 episode run of his podcast *Inkstains* (based on his three-time year-long projects of the same name), Urbancik (pronounced Urban as in City, Sick as in Puppy) has written books like the *DarkWalker* series, *Stale Reality* (also available in Russian), *The Night Carnival,* and *Choose Your Doom.*

Born on a small island in the northeast United States called Manhattan, he is currently sequestered in an undisclosed location in the Pennsylvania woods near the Susquehanna River.

ALSO BY JOHN URBANCIK

NOVELS
Sins of Blood and Stone
Breath of the Moon
Once Upon a Time in Midnight
Stale Reality
The Corpse and the Girl from Miami
DarkWalker 1: Hunting Grounds
DarkWalker 2: Inferno
DarkWalker 3: The Deep City
DarkWalker 4: Armageddon
DarkWalker 5: Ghost Stories
DarkWalker 6: Other Realms
Choose Your Doom

NOVELLAS
A Game of Colors
The Rise and Fall of Babylon (with Brian Keene)
Wings of the Butterfly
House of Shadow and Ash
Necropolis
Quicksilver
Beneath Midnight
Zombies vs. Aliens vs. Robots vs. Cowboys vs.
Ninja vs. Investment Bankers vs. Green Berets
Colette and the Tiger
The Night Carnival
Clockwork Ravens

COLLECTIONS
Shadows, Legends & Secrets
Sound and Vision
Tales of the Fantastic and the Phantasmagoric

POETRY
John the Revelator

NONFICTION
InkStained: On Creativity, Writing, and Art

INKSTAINS
Multiple volumes

Made in the USA
Middletown, DE
26 May 2022

66289724R00076